is invited to a **wedding**

For the Superloves of my life—my family! —C.M.H.

For Kirsten, thank you for all your hard work
and the fun times! —M.C.

Superlove

by
Charise Mericle Harper

illustrated by
Mark Chambers

Alfred A. Knopf
New York

Today I am

Superlove!

There will be **love**,
a wedding,
and happily ever after.

Mommy tries to help me pick out my clothes.

"Oh, Mommy. **Superlove** doesn't wear blue."

Superlove has to look . . . like **love**!

The special wand of love says
who will fall in love.

Today Pinky will
be **married**.

Pinky does not want to get dressed yet.
Maybe later.

Does Superlove eat pancakes for breakfast?
No! Superlove eats
love cakes!

"Thank you, Mommy.
I am filled with
love."

Mommy says,
"Today is a beautiful day to be outside."

She is right.
An outside wedding will be
perfect.

Making a wedding is a lot of work.
And it has to look good, too.
A wedding has to have:

Pretty things hanging down.

A special path to walk on.

Lots of guests.

A place for the
bride and groom
to stand.

And a real, live
Flower girl.

The flower girl is very important.
I will do that part.

I have to use leaves instead of flowers, because Mommy does not think that stems without petals are beautiful.

We have talked about that before.

Pinky is hiding.
She is shy.
Poor Mr. Mittens.
He will have to wait.

I can do some practice weddings first.
That way, everything will be perfect for the
real wedding.

Violet and Bob
get married.

Silver and Spike
get married.

Sabrina and Orcky
get married.

Mimi and Mr. Munchkins
get married.

Now everyone is married except
Pinky and Mr. Mittens.

I try everything, but Pinky will not come down.

Pinky! Pinky!

"You get down here! It's time to get married."

I point my wand,
but it does not work.

Pinky!

Mommy runs out of the house.
"Why are you shouting?" asks Mommy.

"Oh, Mommy.
Pinky is ruining everything!
I can't be a **Plower girl**
if she won't come down
and get married.
She needs to follow me
up the special path."

Mommy looks around and says,
"Wait here. I have an idea."

Mommy is probably going to get some tuna fish.

Tuna fish is a good idea.
Pinky always comes for tuna fish.

Mommy brings Daddy instead,
and no tuna fish.

What can Daddy do? Climb the tree?

"No," says Mommy.
"Daddy and I can get married,
and this time you can be there, too."

The wedding is wonderful!
The groom looks handsome.
The bride looks beautiful.

And the flower girl is
super perfect.

And almost everyone lives
happily ever after.

THIS IS A BORZOI BOOK
PUBLISHED BY ALFRED A. KNOPF

Text copyright © 2014 by
Charise Mericle Harper
Jacket art and interior illustrations
copyright © 2014 by Mark Chambers

All rights reserved. Published in the United States by Alfred A. Knopf, an imprint of Random House Children's Books, a division of Random House LLC, a Penguin Random House Company, New York. Knopf, Borzoi Books, and the colophon are registered trademarks of Random House LLC.

Visit us on the Web! randomhousekids.com

Educators and librarians, for a variety of teaching tools, visit us at RHTeachersLibrarians.com

Library of Congress Cataloging-in-Publication Data
Harper, Charise Mericle. Superlove / Charise Mericle Harper, Mark Chambers. — 1st ed.   p.   cm.
Summary: "A little girl deems herself 'Superlove' and arranges a wedding between her cat, Pinky, and stuffed dog, much to Pinky's dismay." —Provided by publisher
ISBN 978-0-375-86923-5 (trade) — ISBN 978-0-375-96923-2 (lib. bdg.) — ISBN 978-0-375-98726-7 (ebook)
[1. Weddings—Fiction. 2. Love—Fiction. 3. Cats—Fiction. 4. Toys—Fiction.]
I. Chambers, Mark. II. Title. PZ7.H231323Su 2014   [E]—dc23   2012019671

The text of this book is set in 19-point Guardi Roman.
The illustrations were created digitally.

MANUFACTURED IN CHINA
December 2014
10 9 8 7 6 5 4 3 2 1
First Edition